GHOST IN THE HOUSE

GHOST IN THE

HOUSE

Ammi-Joan Paquette

illustrated by
Adam Record

CANDLEWICK PRESS

BOO!

There's a ghost in the house,
In the creepy haunted house,
On this dark, spooky night, all alone.

And he goes slip-slide
With a swoop and a glide
Until suddenly he hears . . .

A GROAN!

And a mummy makes two in the house,

In the creepy haunted house,

On this dark, spooky night, on the prowl.

And they shuffle around
Without even a sound
Until suddenly they hear . . .

A GROWL!

And a monster makes three in the house,
In the creepy haunted house,
On this dark, spooky night, midnight black.

And they creep and crawl
Down the echoing hall
Until suddenly they hear . . .

CLICK-

CLACK!

And a skeleton makes four in the house,
In the creepy haunted house,
On this dark, spooky night, cold and bleak.

And they stagger and stomp
In a spine-chilling romp
Until suddenly they hear . . .

A SHRIEK!

And a witch makes five in the house,

In the creepy haunted house,

On this dark, spooky night — best beware!

Then a sudden FLASH
Makes them topple and crash,
And suddenly they hear . . .

"WHO'S THERE?"

There's a boy in the house,
In the creepy haunted house,
On this dark, spooky night — what a fright!

Five, four, three, two, one —
All the creatures run!
Leaving him alone to say . . .

"GOOD NIGHT!"

For Lils,
in memory of those long-ago days
of "the Es and the As"
A. J. P.

To my kids, Haven and Liam
A. R.

Text copyright © 2013 by Ammi-Joan Paquette
Illustrations copyright © 2013 by Adam Record

First edition 2013

Library of Congress Catalog Card Number 2012943659
ISBN 978-0-7636-5529-7

13 14 15 16 17 18 TLF 10 9 8 7 6 5 4 3 2 1

Printed in Dongguan, Guangdong, China

This book was typeset in Historical Fell Type Roman and Garrotflower.
The illustrations were created digitally.

Candlewick Press
99 Dover Street
Somerville, Massachusetts 02144

visit us at www.candlewick.com